Topsy + Tim

go to the farm

Jean and Gareth Adamson

Blackie

*British Library Cataloguing in Publication Data
Adamson, Jean
Topsy and Tim go to the farm
I. Title   II. Adamson, Gareth
823'.914[J]*

*ISBN 0-216-92463-4
ISBN 0-216-92462-6 Pbk*

*Blackie and Son Limited
7 Leicester Place
London WC2H 7BP*

Printed in Portugal

Topsy and Tim and Mummy were
on their way to Rosemary Farm.
They were going to see Mummy's friend
Mrs Stewart, the farmer's wife.

'May we help on the farm?' asked Topsy.
Mrs Stewart gave them two egg-boxes.
'Go along to the hen-house,' she said,
'and choose twelve nice eggs from the
hens' nests to take home.'

Some hens came to greet Topsy and Tim and a duck quacked cheerfully.

Topsy found some ducklings
learning to swim in an old bath.

A loud hissing noise startled Topsy
and Tim. Three big, angry-looking geese
were moving towards them.
'We'd better run into the hen-house,'
said Tim.

The hen-house felt safe, but it was
very gloomy. Soon their eyes grew used
to the dark and they could see plenty of
eggs in the hens' nests. Topsy chose
six big eggs to fill her box. Four were
white and two were brown.

The angry geese were on the path back
to the farmhouse, so Topsy and Tim
could not go that way. They climbed
the wall instead, being very careful
with their eggs.
'Let's go back to the farmhouse
this way,' said Tim.

Topsy and Tim were in the cows' meadow.
They did not know which way to turn.
Then they saw Farmer Stewart.
'I'm about to take these cows to the
milking-sheds,' said Farmer Stewart.
'Will you give me a hand?'

Topsy and Tim helped Farmer Stewart
take the cows to the milking-sheds,
although the cows knew the way
themselves.

'Can we help milk the cows?' asked Topsy and Tim.
'We will soon do that with our machines, thank you,' said Farmer Stewart. 'I've got a special job for you, though, if you'd care to help.'

Farmer Stewart took a bucket of new milk.
He led Topsy and Tim to a smaller shed.
There was a baby calf in the shed.
'Poor thing. It wants this milk,'
said Farmer Stewart, 'but it can't drink.
It only knows how to suck. Put your eggs
down somewhere and then you can teach
the calf how to drink from the bucket.'

Farmer Stewart showed Topsy what to do.
She dipped her finger in the milk. Then
she let the calf suck her milky finger.
The calf sucked so hard that Topsy felt
nervous.

'Don't worry, it won't bite,' said
Farmer Stewart. Next, Topsy put
her hand into the bucket. The calf
went on sucking Topsy's finger
until her hand and its nose were both
in the warm milk. Then it was Tim's turn
to feed the calf.

The calf soon discovered how to drink
from the bucket without any help.
Topsy and Tim ran back to the
farmhouse to tell Mummy
all about it.

It was time for Topsy and Tim to go home.
As they walked down the lane they heard
a tractor behind them.
It was Farmer Stewart.

'Here are the eggs you forgot,' he said, 'and here is a big carton of cream for your tea, because you were so good and helpful at the farm.'